First published in Great Britain 2022 by Farshore
An imprint of HarperCollins*Publishers*,
1 London Bridge Street, London SE1 9GF
www.farshore.co.uk

HarperCollins*Publishers*, 1st Floor, Watermarque Building, Ringsend Road Dublin 4, Ireland

© 2022 Disney Enterprises, Inc.

ISBN 978 0 0085 0764 0
Printed in Romania
001
A CIP catalogue record for this title is available from the British Library.

Parental guidance is advised for all craft and colouring activities. Always ask an adult to help
when using glue, paint and scissors. Wear protective clothing and cover surfaces to avoid staining.

Stay safe online. Farshore is not responsible for content hosted by third parties.

FSC
www.fsc.org

MIX
Paper from
responsible sources
FSC™ C007454

This **Disney**

FROZEN

ANNUAL 2023

belongs to . . . .
. . . .

Age . . . .

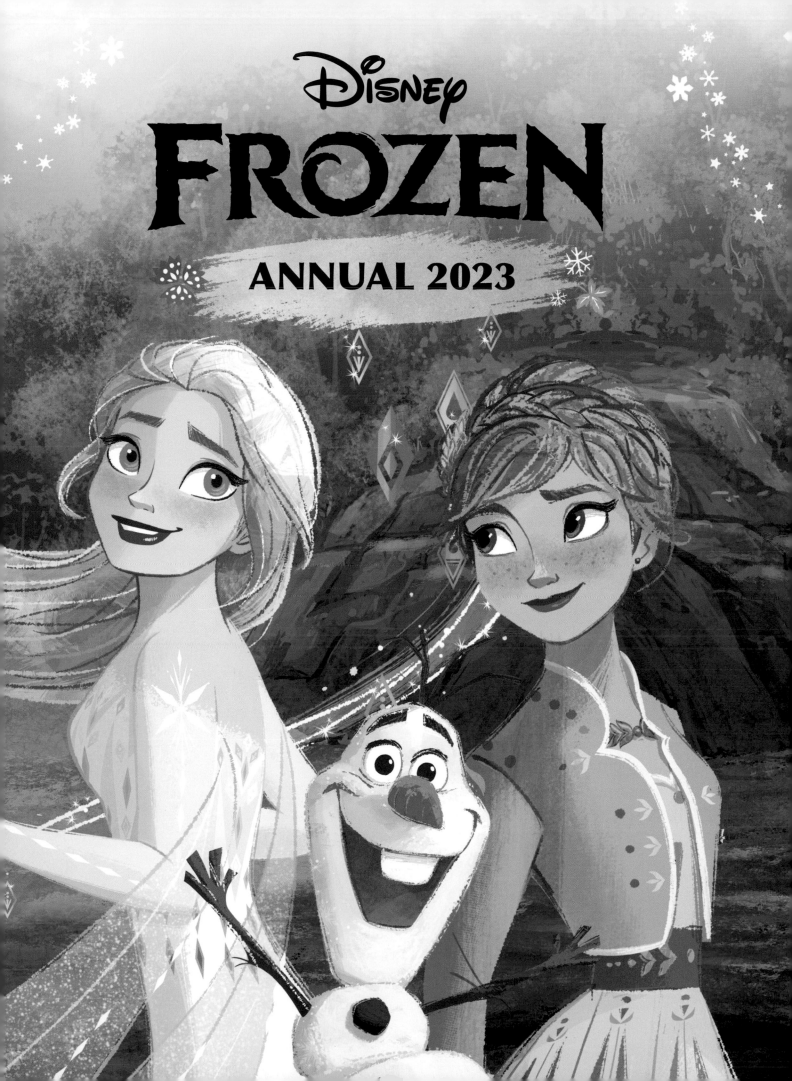

Contents

Frozen Family

Anna, Elsa, Kristoff, Sven and Olaf are the best of friends and have stuck together in their adventures. Meet the magical Frozen family ...

Elsa

Elsa is unique as the only source of magic in Arendelle. Having set her magic free, she is true to herself and embraces her powers.

Anna

Always looking on the bright side, Anna is a fearless adventurer. She will always be there for her friends and family.

Lieutenant Mattias

Having been trapped in the Enchanted Forest for 30 years, Lieutenant Mattias is a loyal protector of Arendelle.

Yelana

As leader of the Northuldra, Yelana is very wise and always listens to nature. She is a fierce protector of her people.

Sven

As Kristoff's best friend, Sven would do anything for him. He is loyal and enjoys a crunchy carrot!

Kristoff

Kristoff always preferred the company of reindeer, until he met Anna. He is a tough ice harvester, but kind and soft on the inside.

Olaf

Olaf is the most lovable snowman in Arendelle. He dreams of sunny days and loves a warm hug with his friends.

Ryder

Ryder loves reindeer just as much as Kristoff! He dreams of venturing out of the Enchanted Forest and exploring the great plains.

Honeymaren

Honeymaren is a brave and peaceful Northuldran. She helps Elsa to discover her family's past.

9

In A Whirlwind

A storm is brewing in the magical Enchanted Forest. Join Elsa and her friends as they enter the forest and work out who is behind this mischief …

Colour in the patterns in the wind and try making up your own designs.

A

E

G

Gusted!

Can you spot the letters scattered in the wind? Collect them to work out who has made these swirling wind shapes.

L

11

Answer on page 68.

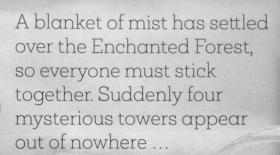

Surrounded by the Mist

A blanket of mist has settled over the Enchanted Forest, so everyone must stick together. Suddenly four mysterious towers appear out of nowhere ...

The Elements

The four symbols on the towers represent each of the elements in nature. Can you match up the correct shape with the symbols below?

EARTH

FIRE

WIND

WATER

1

2

Icy Patterns

Elsa is learning all about the four elements. Help her follow the symbols in the order shown below to find Olaf.

START

FINISH

Who's Missing?

Who is the fifth element that unites all the elements?

a

b

c

Answers on page 68.

Glowing Memories

EVERY YEAR IN THE VALLEY OF THE LIVING ROCK THERE'S A BIG CEREMONY THAT TAKES PLACE UNDER THE NORTHERN LIGHTS. KRISTOFF IS LEADING HIS FRIENDS TO EXPERIENCE THIS MYSTERIOUS TRADITION!

HEY, GUYS!

RUMBLE RUMBLE

POP

THEY'RE HERE!

KRISTOFF! I CAN'T BELIEVE IT'S FINALLY TIME!

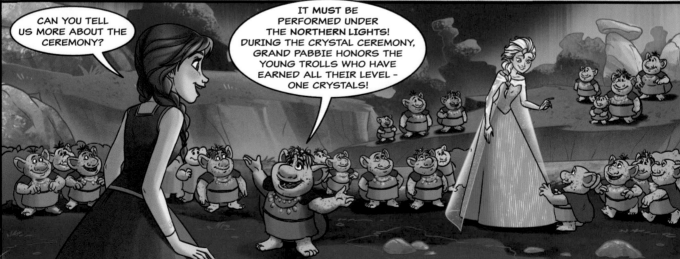

CAN YOU TELL US MORE ABOUT THE CEREMONY?

IT MUST BE PERFORMED UNDER THE NORTHERN LIGHTS! DURING THE CRYSTAL CEREMONY, GRAND PABBIE HONORS THE YOUNG TROLLS WHO HAVE EARNED ALL THEIR LEVEL - ONE CRYSTALS!

Adapted from Disney Frozen books A New Beginning, On the Trail, and Let It Glow, written by Suzanne Francis; manuscript adaptation by Francesca Frigo; layout: Benedetta Barone; cleanup: Benedetta Barone; color: MAAWillustration

SO OUR FRIENDS VENTURE THROUGH THE FOREST, LOOKING FOR GRAND PABBIE ...

TROLLS HAVE AN INCREDIBLE SENSE OF SMELL! I THINK IT'S GRAND PABBIE!

ERM ...

SNIFF SNIFF

UM, THAT'S ... SVEN.

SVEN! STOP STANDING ON GRAND PABBIE'S FOOTPRINTS!

!

WE SHOULD GO THIS WAY!

PAY ATTENTION: I DON'T KNOW HOW SOLID THE ICE IS!

DON'T WORRY! I DID EARN MY ICE TREKKING CRYSTAL AND ... OOPS!

CRACK

Bright Night Sky

Kristoff and Sven have shared many magical memories together. Make this moment extra special and add the Northern Lights above them. Try using yellow, blue, pink, green and purple pencils.

Frosty Beginnings

Take a trip back to Wandering Oaken's Trading Post, where Anna and Kristoff first met. Can you spot the 5 differences between these pictures?

1

2

Answers on page 68.

Reach for the Sky

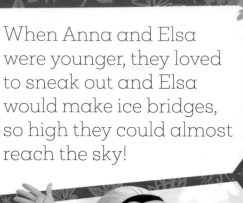

When Anna and Elsa were younger, they loved to sneak out and Elsa would make ice bridges, so high they could almost reach the sky!

33	34 Go down the slide!	35
32	31	
Climb up the stairs!	18	19
16 Go down the slide!	15	Climb up the stairs!
1		3

START

22

How to play:

- This is a game for two players.
- You'll need a dice and two counters.
- Place your tokens on the START space.
- Take turns rolling the dice and moving the number of spaces shown.
- If you land at the bottom of an ice staircase, move your counter up.
- If you land on top of a slide, move your token down.
- The first player to reach the FINISH wins!

FINISH

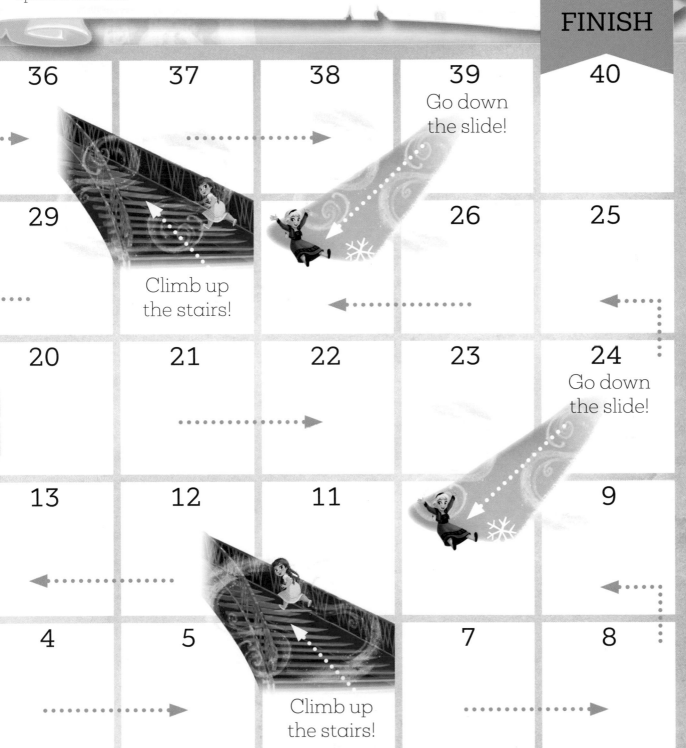

36	37	38	39 Go down the slide!	40
29	Climb up the stairs!		26	25
20	21	22	23	24 Go down the slide!
13	12	11		9
4	5	Climb up the stairs!	7	8

23

Odd One Out

Anna is always up for an adventure, but she needs to come prepared. Can you tell which of these pictures of Anna is the odd one out?

Answer on page 68.

Into the
Unknown

Starry Nights

While Anna and Olaf are stargazing, they can see some shapes in the stars. Connect the numbered dots to find out what shapes they can see.

leaf shoti he bear

Answers on page 68.

Glowing Memories

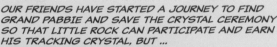

OUR FRIENDS HAVE STARTED A JOURNEY TO FIND GRAND PABBIE AND SAVE THE CRYSTAL CEREMONY SO THAT LITTLE ROCK CAN PARTICIPATE AND EARN HIS TRACKING CRYSTAL, BUT ...

WHAT IF A GIANT BIRD CARRIED GRAND PABBIE OFF, OR MAYBE HE GOT INTO A FIGHT WITH A SQUIRREL?

AND WHAT IF A SWARM OF ANGRY BUTTERFLIES JUST ... JUST ... *GOBBLED* HIM UP!

LITTLE ROCK, THERE ARE NO BIRDS STRONG ENOUGH TO PICK UP GRAND PABBIE. SQUIRRELS ARE FRIENDLY TOWARD TROLLS, AND BUTTERFLIES, EVEN WHEN THEY'RE ANGRY, LIKE TO EAT POLLEN!

TE-HE-HE, YOU'RE RIGHT ...

ER ... SORRY TO INTERRUPT, BUT ...

RUMBLE RUMBLE

WE MAY HAVE A PROBLEM! A STORM IS COMING!

I'LL TAKE CARE OF THIS!

Adapted from Disney Frozen books *A New Beginning*, *On the Trail*, and *Let It Glow*, written by Suzanne Francis; manuscript adaptation by Francesca Frigo; layout: Benedetta Barone; cleanup: Benedetta Barone; color: MAAWillustration

WE MAY BE HERE FOR A LITTLE WHILE!

WELL ... HOW ABOUT A STORY?

AW! I LOVE STORIES! WHO HAS A STORY TO TELL?

HOW ABOUT A STORY FROM BACK WHEN I WAS YOUNG?

YEEEEAH!

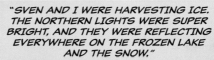

"SVEN AND I WERE HARVESTING ICE. THE NORTHERN LIGHTS WERE SUPER BRIGHT, AND THEY WERE REFLECTING EVERYWHERE ON THE FROZEN LAKE AND THE SNOW."

"SVEN WAS GOING CRAZY TRYING TO CATCH THE REFLECTIONS, AND HE FINALLY CAUGHT ONE ..."

" ... WITH HIS TONGUE!"

"I TRIED PULLING AND PUSHING HIM, BUT NOTHING WORKED, UNTIL I HAD AN IDEA ..."

I'LL GET YOU OUT OF THIS, SVEN!

"THAT WAS QUITE AN ADVENTURE, BUT IN THE END WE DID IT!"

YOU ALWAYS HAVE SUCH GREAT STORIES. I WISH I HAD A GOOD STORY TO TELL, TOO!

I'M SURE YOU HAVE LOTS OF GREAT STORIES, EVEN IF YOU DON'T KNOW IT YET!

IT LOOKS LIKE THE WIND HAS STOPPED! LET'S GET BACK ON TRACK!

WOOOOW! I NEVER KNEW MOUNTAINS COULD BE THIS **MAGICAL** AND—

THIS IS UNBELIEVABLE! LOOK!

HEY! THIS IS GRAND PABBIE'S!

SNIFF SNIFF

HE MUST HAVE DROPPED IT AS HE CLIMBED THE CLIFF!

BUT HOW ARE **WE** GOING TO CLIMB IT? THE CURRENT IS TOO STRONG!

!

WHAT AN IDEA, SVEN! HE SUGGESTS ELSA FREEZES THE WATERFALL!

SO WE CAN CLIMB IT!

THIS SHOULD DO.

YAY! I'VE ALWAYS WANTED TO CLIMB A FROZEN WATERFALL!

BE CAREFUL!

I'VE TOTALLY GOT THIS!

THIS IS GOING TO BE SO MUCH FUN!

OKAY, GUYS, WE'LL LIFT YOU UP. AND, ELSA, YOU'RE NEXT!

!

SWOOOSH

WHY DIDN'T YOU DO THAT IN THE FIRST PLACE?

YOU WERE SO EXCITED THAT I DIDN'T WANT TO SPOIL ANYONE'S FUN!

FINALLY ...

LOOK! ISN'T THAT ...?

I FOUND HIM!

HELLO, LITTLE ROCK!

MY CRYSTAL IS STILL DULL. I GUESS I'M NOT VERY GOOD AT TRACKING AND I NEVER WOULD HAVE FOUND YOU WITHOUT MY FRIENDS! AND ...

BUT ...

HOW IS THAT POSSIBLE? I DIDN'T EARN IT!

GASP!

ACTUALLY, YOU DID, BY REALIZING YOU NEEDED HELP AND WORKING WITH YOUR FRIENDS!

NOW, IT'S TIME FOR THE CEREMONY TO BEGIN!

SO ...

IT LOOKS LIKE I HAVE A STORY TO TELL AFTER ALL!

A MAGICAL ADVENTURE YOU'LL REMEMBER FOREVER!

The End

The Gates are Open!

The cakes have been made, the halls are decorated, now it's time to welcome guests into the castle! Everyone is welcome in Arendelle.

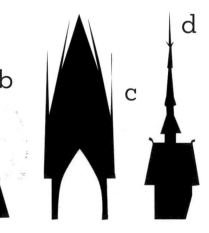

Stately Shapes

Arendelle Castle is very big, with many towers, windows and rooms. Can you match the silhouette to the correct part of the castle?

Go Inside

Anna has left something in each of these rooms. Can you help her find the item in each room? Tick the box next to the object you've found.

a 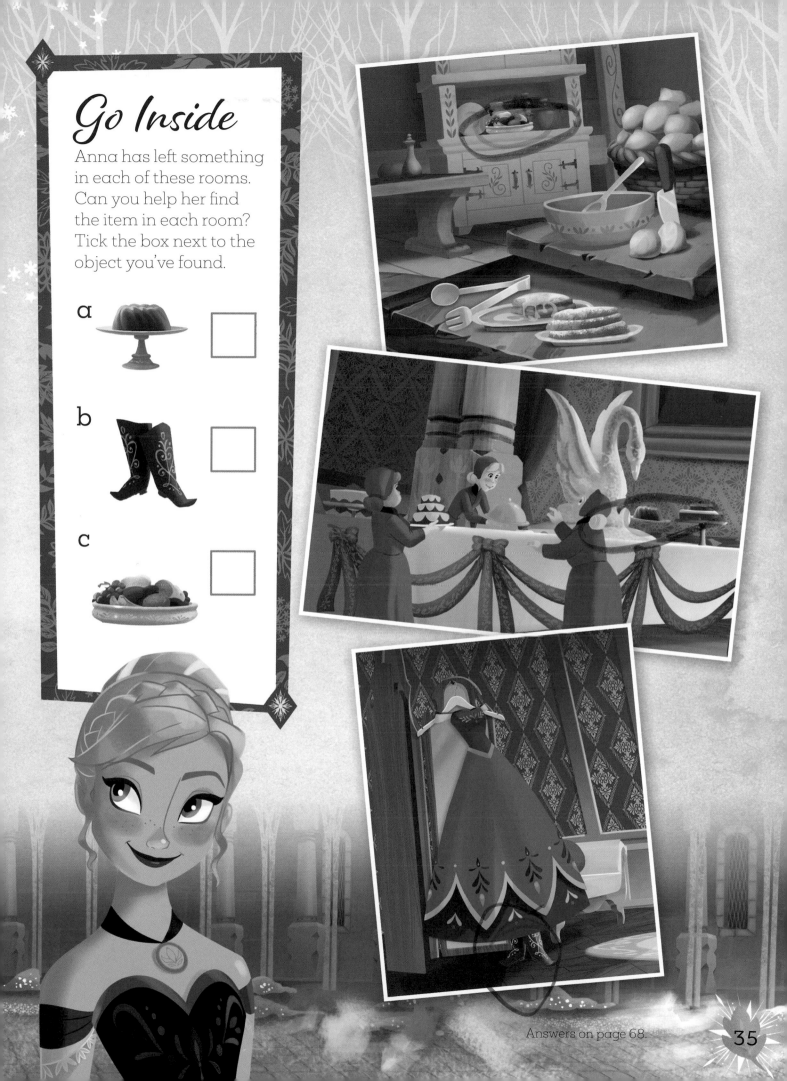 ☐

b ☐

c ☐

Winter Market

Everyone in Arendelle has gathered for the Winter Market! But it's easy to get lost among the crowds …

Can you find the images below? Tick the boxes as you do.

Answers on page 68.

Outdoor Lessons

Anna and Olaf are inspired by the nature of Arendelle whilst Olaf learns to read and count. Can you help him complete the activities below?

Reading Lines

This is the sequence.

Olaf loves books! Follow the correct sequence in the grid to help him in his studies. You can move horizontally and vertically.

START

FINISH

Nature Watch

Can you help Olaf count the butterflies?

| 5 | 4 | 3 |

There are 8L butterflies in total.

Answers on page 69.

Family Fun

Anna, Elsa, Olaf, Kristoff and Sven love each other so much! Use your crayons to colour in this picture of the five of them together.

A New Look

NOT LONG AFTER THE CORONATION, ANNA IS PREPARING FOR THE DAY ...

I LOVE YOUR NEW DRESS, ANNA!

ME TOO! THE CORONATION DRESS WAS GETTING A LITTLE CUMBERSOME AND I NEEDED SOMETHING FOR EVERYDAY.

Script by Valentina Cambi; layout: Emilio Urbano; cleanup: Letizia Algeri; color: Dario Calabria

IT'S COMFORTABLE AND NOT TOO BIG ...

I REALLY FEEL GOOD IN IT!

I'D ALSO LIKE TO HAVE A NEW LOOK ...

WHAT IF I CHANGED MY NOSE?

YOUR NOSE?

I'M SURE I COULD FIND SOMETHING MORE UNIQUE THAN A CARROT ...

HAVE YOU FOUND ANY INSPIRATION YET, OLAF?

NOT YET ...

HEY, GUYS! MAKING BIG DECISIONS?

WELL, KIND OF ...

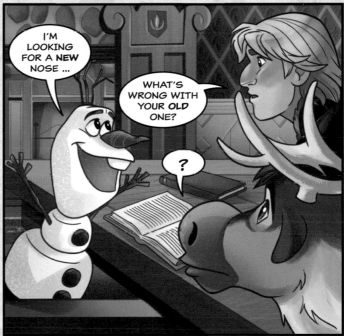

I'M LOOKING FOR A NEW NOSE ...

WHAT'S WRONG WITH YOUR OLD ONE?

?

ALL THE SNOWMEN HAVE A CARROT NOSE! I WANT SOMETHING DIFFERENT ...

OKAY, WHAT ABOUT A COURGETTE OR A CUCUMBER OR BROCCOLI?

OH, NO ... NOT A VEGETABLE!

43

GOOD! AT LEAST WE HAVE A **START**! WHAT ELSE, OLAF?

HUMANS AND ANIMALS CAN USE THEIR NOSES TO SMELL ...

SNIFF SNIFF

I'D LIKE MINE TO BE USEFUL, TOO!

I GOT IT!

THIS **CANDLE** IS JUST PERFECT! I CAN USE IT TO READ AT NIGHT!

HEHE! VERY USEFUL!

NO! VERY DANGEROUS!

WHOOOAAA!!!

WHOOSH

I'M SORRY ...
I RUINED THE
BOOK!

DON'T
WORRY. THE PAGE
IS ONLY SLIGHTLY
DAMAGED.

TOO
BAD ABOUT THE
LEMONADE ...

HAHA!

SLURP
SLURP

WELL
DONE, MY
FRIEND!

OLAF JUST GOT A NEW IDEA ...

WHAT IF
I COULD HAVE A
NOSE MADE OF CAKE?
THAT WAY I WOULD ALWAYS
SMELL SOMETHING
GOOD!

SWEET
IDEA!

I NEED
OLINA'S HELP!

WAIT, OLAF!
WE'LL GO WITH
YOU!

OLAF IS PROUD OF HIS NEW LOOK!

YOU LOOK NICE!

I LOVE KRUMKAKES! I COULDN'T FIND A BETTER NOSE ...

AND YOU'RE NOT THE ONLY ONE WHO LOVES THEM!

WOOF WOOF WOOF

I THINK HE'S LOOKING FOR A SNACK ...

UH?

LICK

HERE YOU ARE!

SLURP!

SOON AFTER, OLAF GETS A NEW NOSE ...

HERE'S ANOTHER KRUMKAKE FOR YOU!

THANK YOU, OLINA!

BUT ...

WOOF WOOF WOOF

I'M SURE YOUR NOSE IS VERY DELICIOUS, OLAF!

?!

BUT I'M AFRAID YOU SHOULD FIND ANOTHER ONE IF YOU DON'T WANT TO KEEP CHANGING IT!

SHORTLY AFTER ...

HOW IS IT GOING WITH THIS NOSE?

FANTASTIC! WE'RE GOING NORTH!

WAIT! NOW WE'RE HEADING EAST ...

HEY! WE'RE CHANGING DIRECTION AGAIN ...

UH-OH ... MY HEAD IS SPINNING!

YOU CAN'T KEEP LOOKING AT THE COMPASS, OLAF!

THE NEEDLE MOVES TOO FAST AND YOU GET DIZZY!

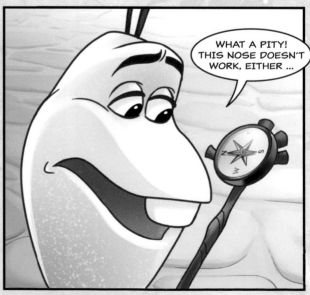

WHAT A PITY! THIS NOSE DOESN'T WORK, EITHER ...

OOH! OAKEN'S KIOSK!

I FEEL EXACTLY LIKE WHEN I WAS IN HIS STORE, AFTER ELSA CREATED ME. I REMEMBER TRYING ON A LOT OF DIFFERENT NOSES! AND THE LAST WAS A SAUSAGE ...

BUT WHEN WE MET YOU, YOU DIDN'T HAVE A NOSE ...

I GAVE THE SAUSAGE TO A HUNGRY WOLF ALONG THE WAY!

SO I PUT THIS **CARROT** ON YOUR FACE!

IT WAS SUCH A **GREAT** FEELING!

YOU ARE **UNIQUE** AND **ORIGINAL** AS YOU ARE!

YOU HAVE NO NEED TO CHANGE YOUR LOOK, OLAF!

YOU'RE RIGHT, ANNA! THIS IS EXACTLY THE NOSE I HAVE ALWAYS **LIKED**!

The End

You're Special!

Olaf has learned that he is special just the way he is. And so are you!

Royal Portrait

Imagine you are royalty, sitting for your royal portrait. Draw a picture of yourself, and make sure to add a crown!

Build a Snowman

Rearrange the jumbled pieces to match the picture of Olaf. Write the numbers in the blank squares.

Answers on page 69.

5

1

Discovering the Elements

The spirits of the Enchanted Forest are magical beings in nature. They include water, fire, wind and earth. Elsa is the fifth element that unites them all. Can you help her find the names of the elements?

GALE   ELSA   NOKK
GIANT   BRUNI

T	N	G	A	I	K	D	B
U	A	N	X	K	J	I	R
T	O	Q	O	I	H	G	U
N	L	D	S	K	A	H	N
A	I	O	T	T	K	E	I
I	H	W	B	O	D	Z	Y
G	A	L	E	O	W	D	I
R	Q	V	E	L	S	A	P

Answers on page 69.

Into the Unknown

Elsa can hear the mysterious voice calling to her from Ahtohallan. Can you help her find the way through the maze to it?

START

FINISH

Woodland Trail

Anna and Olaf have become separated in the Enchanted Forest. Can you work out which path will help Anna reach Olaf?

PATH 1

PATH 2

PATH 3

PATH 4

FINISH

54

Answer on page 69.

Charades

Olaf always wins a game of charades! Can you work out what he is in each picture below? Draw lines to match each picture to the right word.

a

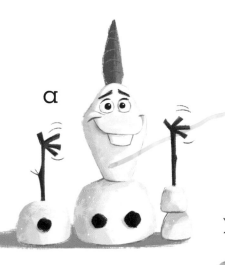

b

unicorn

ice cream

rabbit

c

sandcastle

Oaken

d

e

Answers on page 69.

Forest Friends

B

A

Coming Together

It's a big moment when the Northuldra and Arendelliens come together. Can you match the jigsaw pieces to the spaces in the picture? Write the letters by the pieces to complete this puzzle.

Answers on page 69.

The Road to Peace

Lieutenant Mattias and Yelana have put their differences aside. Find the right path that joins Mattias to Yelana.

1

2

3

Answer on page 69.

A Brave Girl

IT'S A RAINY EVENING IN ARENDELLE, THE PERFECT MOMENT FOR STORIES BY THE FIREPLACE ...

... A FLASH OF LIGHTNING RIPPED THROUGH THE SKY, FOLLOWED BY A LOUD CRASH OF THUNDER.

I WAS SO SCARED THAT I COULDN'T SLEEP ...

THEN MY MOTHER CAME. SHE SAT NEXT TO ME, WRAPPED THIS **SCARF** AROUND MY SHOULDERS, AND ...

OH, IT'S SO WARM!

Script by: Tea Orsi; Layout Emilio Urbano; Clean Manuela Razzi; Color: MAAWIllustration

... SUDDENLY. ALL MY FEARS **DISAPPEARED**!

REALLY?

SO YOUR SCARF SENDS ALL YOUR FEARS AWAY? EVEN THE BIGGEST ONES?

ALL OF THEM, MY DEAR. IT IS FULL OF **LOVE** AND MEMORIES, WHICH WILL ALWAYS MAKE YOU FEEL AT HOME.

ELSA, HAVE YOU SEEN ANNA? SHE'S NOT IN HER ROOM.

I THOUGHT SHE WAS WITH YOU, MOTHER.

MAYBE SHE'S IN THE **LIBRARY** WITH FATHER ...

GOOD IDEA. LET'S GO CHECK!

BUT ...

AGNARR, WE ARE LOOKING FOR ANNA ...

I THINK SHE'S BEEN HERE, BECAUSE I FOUND THIS **DRAWING**.

IT'S US! MAYBE IT'S A **MESSAGE** FROM HER.

BUT ... WHY IS SHE **MISSING** FROM THIS FAMILY PORTRAIT?

I DON'T KNOW, BUT I THINK SHE WANTS US TO **KEEP LOOKING** FOR HER.

WHERE COULD SHE BE? WE SEARCHED ALL THE ROOMS IN THE CASTLE.

BUT WE DIDN'T CHECK THE COURTYARD. I'LL GET MY SCARF AND GO OUTSIDE!

BUT INSTEAD OF THE SCARF, IDUNA FINDS SOMETHING ELSE ...

ANOTHER DRAWING FROM ANNA?!

IT'S A MONSTER! WHAT DOES THIS MEAN?

A MONSTER IS SCARY. MAYBE ANNA WANTS TO LET US KNOW THAT SHE'S **SOMEWHERE** SHE'S AFRAID OF ...

I KNOW! SHE MUST BE IN THE **ATTIC**!

BUT SHE NEVER GOES UP THERE ALONE ...

SHE MADE THOSE DRAWINGS BECAUSE SHE WANTS US TO **FIND** HER!

Take the Test

1. What is the name of the fire spirit?
   a. Gale
   b. Bruni
   c. Leo

2. What is Anna and Elsa's mother's name?
   a. Iduna
   b. India
   c. Irina

3. Where do Anna and Kristoff meet for the first time?
   a. Enchanted Forest
   b. Oaken's Trading Post
   c. Arendelle Market

4. Who was King Agnarr's official guard?
   a. Yelana
   b. Prince Hans
   c. Lieutenant Mattias

5. What is Kristoff's job?
   a. Ice Harvester
   b. Carrot Seller
   c. Painter

6. Who is the Northuldra leader?
   a. Honeymaren
   b. Sven
   c. Yelana

7. What keeps Olaf from melting?
   a. Large fan
   b. Personal flurry
   c. Giant freezer

8. Where do the trolls live?
   a. The moon
   b. The Valley of the Living Rock
   c. The Enchanted Forest

9. Who loves reindeer just as much as Kristoff?
   a. Ryder
   b. Honeymarren
   c. Anna

10. Where does the Water Nokk take Elsa?
    a. Enchanted Forest
    b. Arendelle
    c. Ahtohallan

How did you do?

8-10 Expert!
You really know your ice queens from your ice creams! Well done.

4-7 Great.
Nearly there. Another journey into Arendelle should do the trick.

0-3 Ahto-what-an?
Don't worry, you'll just have to read the annual again!

Answers on page 69.

Some Things
Never Change!

We Belong
Together

Sister Connection

Anna and Elsa will always have each other's back. They love each other so much! Use your crayons to colour in this picture and bring the sisterly love to life.

Blast from the Past

Elsa and Anna have been on lots of adventures. Trace over the words to bring back the memories.

ice

queen

snow

castle

love

Think about your favourite characters in the Frozen films and draw them.

Answers

PAGE 10 *In A Whirlwind*

GALE is behind the winds.

PAGE 12 *Surrounded by the Mist*

The Elements

1. WATER
2. WIND
3. FIRE
4. EARTH

Icy Patterns

Who's Missing?

c – Elsa

PAGE 21 *Frosty Beginnings*

PAGE 24 *Odd One Out*

Image 4 is the odd one out.

PAGE 27 *Starry Nights*

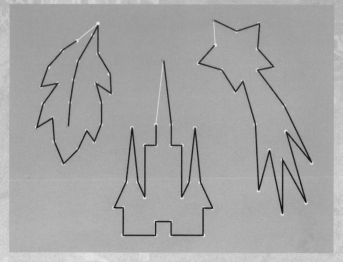

PAGE 34 *The Gates are Open!*

Stately Shapes

1 – d, 2 – b, 3 – c, 4 – a.

Go Inside

PAGE 36 *Winter Market*

68

PAGE 38 *Outdoor Lessons*

Reading Lines

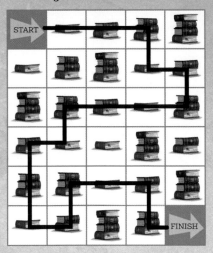

Nature Watch

5 yellow butterflies
4 red butterflies
3 blue butterflies
12 butterflies in total

PAGE 50 *You're Special!*

Build a Snowman

1
2
3
4
5

PAGE 52 *Discovering the Elements*

T	N	G	A	I	K	D	B
U	A	N	X	K	J	I	R
T	O	Q	O	I	H	G	U
N	L	D	S	K	A	H	N
A	I	O	T	T	K	E	I
I	H	W	B	O	D	Z	Y
G	A	L	E	O	W	D	I
R	Q	V	E	L	S	A	P

PAGE 53 *Into the Unknown*

PAGE 54 *Woodland Trail*

Path 4 leads to Olaf.

PAGE 55 *Charades*

a – sandcastle
b – Oaken
c – ice cream
d – unicorn
e – rabbit

PAGE 56 *Forest Friends*

Coming Together

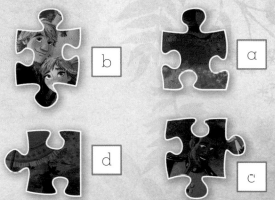

b

a

d

c

The Road to Peace

Path 3 joins Mattias to Yelana.

PAGE 62 *Take the Tests*

1. b – Bruni
2. a – Iduna
3. b – Oaken's Trading Post
4. c – Lieutenant Mattias
5. a – Ice Harvester
6. c – Yelana
7. b – Personal flurry
8. b – The Valley of the Living Rock
9. a – Ryder
10. c – Ahtohallan